# I'm a Narwhal

By Mallory C. Loehr
Illustrated by Joey Chou

A GOLDEN BOOK • NEW YORK

Text copyright © 2019 by Mallory C. Loehr
Cover art and interior illustrations copyright © 2019 by Joey Chou
All rights reserved. Published in the United States by Golden Books, an imprint of Random House
Children's Books, a division of Penguin Random House LLC, 1745 Broadway, New York, NY 10019.
Golden Books, A Golden Book, A Little Golden Book, the G colophon, and the distinctive
gold spine are registered trademarks of Penguin Random House LLC.
rhcbooks.com
Educators and librarians, for a variety of teaching tools, visit us at
RHTeachersLibrarians.com
Library of Congress Control Number: 2018937786
ISBN 978-0-525-64576-4 (trade) — ISBN 978-0-525-64577-1 (ebook)
Printed in the United States of America
10 9 8 7 6 5 4

I am **NOT** a unicorn.

I am NOT a fish.

I'm a **narwhal!**

I look magical,
but I'm really just
a kind of whale.

My closest relatives
are the beluga whale,
the dolphin,
and the porpoise.

I live in the cold Arctic waters
with my pod, or family.

I can dive very deep
and hold my breath
under the ice for a long time!

In the spring, narwhals
swim to warmer bays.
This is called migration.

Once there, we like to lie on
the water's surface and rest.
This is called logging!

Long ago, when narwhal horns
were found on the beach,

people thought they were
magical unicorn horns.

Wouldn't you?

My horn is actually
a big front tooth, or tusk.
It grows in a spiral—
right through my upper lip!

It helps me "taste" the salt
in the water
and find the right places to hunt.

Boy narwhals are usually
the ones with tusks,
but some girls have them, too!

Because I'm a narwhal,
I can stun a tasty codfish
or squid with my tusk—
then suck the meal into my mouth!

I communicate with clicking and knocking sounds.

Humans don't know
what I'm saying,
but my friends and family do!

I may not be a unicorn, but I am magical in my own way ...